This book has been donated
to the students of
Three Creeks Elementary

by
*Members of the Lowell
Lions Club*

September 1990

101
QUESTIONS AND
ANSWERS ABOUT
PETS AND
PEOPLE

101

QUESTIONS AND ANSWERS ABOUT

PETS AND

PEOPLE

DR. ANN SQUIRE

Vice President for Education at the American Society for the Prevention of Cruelty to Animals

ILLUSTRATED BY G. BRIAN KARAS

Macmillan Publishing Company   New York
Collier Macmillan Publishers   London

10   9   8   7   6   5   4   3   2   1

The text of this book is set in 12 point Plantin Light.
The illustrations are rendered in pen-and-ink.

Library of Congress Cataloging-in-Publication Data
Squire, Ann. 101 questions and answers about pets and people/by Ann Squire;
illustrated by G. Brian Karas. — 1st ed.   p.   cm.   Includes index.
Summary: Answers questions about the behavior, requirements, and physical characteristics of pets in such categories as dogs and cats, birds, fish, and pets who help people.

ISBN 0-02-786580-0

1. Pets—Miscellanea—Juvenile literature. [1. Pets—Miscellanea. 2. Questions and
answers.] I. Karas, G. Brian, ill. II. Title. III. One hundred one questions and
answers about pets and people. IV. Title: One hundred and one questions and answers
about pets and people.
SF416.2.S62   1988   636.08'87—dc 19   87-36457   CIP   AC

ACKNOWLEDGMENTS

My sincere thanks to the following people for their help in compiling questions for the book: Al Odmark; Jill Gibson and her students at Star Elementary School in Star, Idaho; Gwen Dewey and the students at the Woodland School in Puyallup, Washington. And thanks most of all to Karen Gravelle, Jeff Squire, and Bunny Squire for the various forms of encouragement each provided.

TO MY PARENTS

CONTENTS

ONE Dogs and Cats

1.
Why are dogs so much more friendly than cats?

Most people would describe dogs as friendly and outgoing and cats as aloof and reserved. These personality differences can be traced back to the ancestors of today's domestic pets. Dogs are the descendants of wolves, which are social animals that live in packs. Within the pack, each member knows its place in relation to the others. The most important pack member is the leader, or "alpha" wolf. Other wolves look to the leader for direction and treat him with respect, which is often shown by licking or nuzzling. So when your dog jumps up and licks your face, it may just be thinking of you as its alpha wolf.

The ancestors of today's domestic cats, on the other hand, lived and hunted alone. Because of this, they did not need to develop the social behaviors necessary for life in a pack. This is why cats seem more independent and less friendly than dogs.

2.
How do cats see so well in the dark?

Cats are natural hunters, and they often prey on rats, mice, and other animals that are active at night. To hunt successfully, cats must be able to see and stalk their prey even on very dark nights. Cats see at least six times better in the dark than people do, and they have the best night vision of all domestic species. Contrary to popular belief, however, cats cannot see in total darkness.

One reason that cats see so well in the dark is because their eyes are so big. In fact, the cat has about the biggest eye (in proportion to its body weight) of any mammal. Another reason is that the cat's retina (the light-sensitive part of the eye) contains many cells that are very active in dim light.

Cats also have a special layer of cells at the back of the eye that makes their eyes even more sensitive to light. When light hits the eye, these cells act as a mirror, reflecting light back through the retina. Because the eye is getting a "double dose" of light (direct and reflected), very little light is necessary for good vision.

These mirrorlike cells also cause a cat's eyes to shine in the dark.

3.
When was the dog domesticated?

Scientists think the dog was the first species to be domesticated by humans. Fossil remains of dogs dating back to the Mesolithic period, twelve thousand years ago, have been found in Israel and Iraq. In this country, canine fossils estimated to be ten thousand years old have been uncovered at an archaeological site called Jaguar Cave in Idaho.

No one really knows why dogs were domesticated, but scientists have some ideas. When domestication occurred, humans were gradually giving up their wandering, nomadic life-styles and settling down into permanent communities. Some scientists think that wild dogs started to spend time near these settlements looking for food, and were at first tolerated and finally accepted by humans.

Other people think that humans deliberately tamed dogs to serve as guards or to help with hunting. One of the most popular theories, though, is that people domesticated dogs simply because they liked them and wanted their companionship. Their useful qualities, such as being good watchdogs, may have been discovered only after they had already become pets.

4.
Why do dogs come in so many different shapes and sizes, while most cats look and act almost alike?

The answer to this puzzling question is selective breeding. As humans domesticated the dog, they began to see that dogs could help them in a number of ways—as guards, hunters, sheepherders, workers, and just as pets. But these different jobs required dogs with different body types and different personalities. For example, a working dog must be large, strong, and patient. A hunting dog must be a fast runner and have good vision and hearing. Dogs used mostly as indoor pets should be small and sociable around people. So, starting with the basic dog (which looked a lot like a wolf), people began to select the look and personality they wanted and breed only the dogs that showed those traits. After many years of selective breeding, we have over one hundred different breeds of dog in the United States alone, including Saint Bernards (rescue dogs), Shetland sheepdogs (herding dogs), Siberian huskies (sled dogs), bloodhounds (tracking dogs), and many more. Not only do different breeds of dog look very different, but each is suited to a particular kind of work.

Cats, on the other hand, are kept mostly as pets and have never been expected to do any specialized work, except catch mice. Because of this, people have had little reason to select for different personalities and body types.

This is why most breeds of cat look and act pretty much the same.

5.
What is the biggest breed of dog?

The answer to that question depends on whether you're talking about weight or height. The heaviest dog is probably the mastiff, which can weigh over two hundred pounds. It is not surprising that mastiffs were originally bred to be watchdogs. The ancient Romans also used them to fight bears, lions, and tigers! In spite of their size, most mastiffs are gentle and friendly.

The tallest dog is the Irish wolfhound, which measures up to three and one-half feet tall at the shoulder when standing on all fours. On its hind legs, the Irish wolfhound can stand over seven feet tall—bigger than most people. As its name suggests, the Irish wolfhound was originally used to hunt wolves in Ireland.

If you are thinking of getting one of these breeds (or any other very large dog, such as a Saint Bernard, Newfoundland, or Great Dane) as a pet, you should make sure you have enough space for the animal to exercise. Big dogs are usually not very happy in apartments or in houses with small backyards. You must also have enough strength to walk your dog, and enough money to feed it—the biggest breeds will eat several hundred dollars' worth of food each year!

6.
What is the smallest breed of dog?

The smallest dog in the world is the "teacup Chihuahua," which weighs less than one pound and can stand in the palm of a person's hand. Even a normal-size Chihuahua is very tiny, weighing between four and six pounds.

The ancestor of the modern Chihuahua is a breed called the Techichi, which was developed in Mexico by the Toltecs almost one thousand years ago. The Techichi was very important in the religious ceremonies of the Toltecs and the Aztecs. It was the Aztec custom, whenever a person died, to sacrifice one of these dogs and bury it with the person. The Aztecs believed that the dog would lead the human soul through the underworld, fighting off evil spirits.

For their size, Chihuahuas have a loud bark and can be very bold and aggressive.

7.
When was the cat domesticated?

Compared to the dog, the domestic cat has been around for a fairly short time—only about fifty-five hundred years. Scientists think that the first domestic cat appeared in Egypt around 3500 B.C. Its ancestors are believed to have been *Felis libyca*, a small spotted wildcat from North Africa, and *Felis sylvestris*, a European wildcat.

Some people think that the Egyptians domesticated the cat for religious reasons. Others believe that the cat was popular because of its superior mouse-catching abilities.

Whatever the Egyptians' original reason for domesticating the cat, it was probably the ability to catch rodents that was responsible for the spread of cats to other parts of the world. People found that cats were very useful in keeping their grain stores free of rats and mice. In the fifth century A.D., barbarian invaders swept across Europe, bringing with them hordes of rats. The cat became people's ally in fighting disease by keeping the rat population in check.

Cats became so valuable that in A.D. 936 the Welsh prince Howell the Good passed laws setting the worth of cats. Not surprisingly, a cat was worth more if it was a good mouser. Prince Howell decreed that a kitten was worth one pence. A grown cat that had not yet caught a mouse was worth only two pence; but after it had learned to catch mice, its value rose to four pence. If someone bought a cat that turned out to be a poor mouser, the buyer was entitled to one-third of the money back.

It was not until 1750 that the first cats were officially imported into the American colonies for the purpose of controlling rodents. Today the cat is the most popular pet in the United States. Over 50 million of them are kept as pets by people across America.

8.
Why are there so many Egyptian statues in the shape of cats?

The Egyptians not only domesticated the cat, but also worshipped it as a goddess. Bastet, the Egyptian goddess of motherhood and fertility, took the shape of a cat. Every young Egyptian couple kept a statue of Bastet in their home, for they believed that this would ensure them many children. Every year, a huge festival in honor of Bastet was held in the city of Bubastis. It is thought that as many as 700,000 people traveled to Bubastis from all over Egypt to take part in the celebrations.

Real cats were associated with the goddess Bastet and, because of this, were treated very well. Anyone who killed a cat was guilty of a crime punishable by death. It was considered quite unlucky to come upon a dead cat in the street. Whoever did so would beat his chest and cry loudly to let others know the animal's death was not his fault.

The death of a pet cat was also a sad occasion, and the

family members showed their grief by shaving off their eyebrows. Cats were given real funerals, and even the poorest Egyptian family made sure the cat had had a decent burial. The pet cats of wealthy Egyptians were often mummified and laid to rest with jeweled collars. Sometimes saucers of milk and mummified mice were placed in the tomb along with the cat so it would have something to eat during its afterlife.

The practice of mummifying cats was very common. In the middle of the nineteenth century, archaeologists found over 300,000 cat mummies in a cemetery in Egypt.

9.
What is the function of a cat's whiskers?

These long hairs growing out of the upper lip, cheeks, and forehead of a cat are actually sense organs. When something touches the tip of a cat's whisker, sensitive nerve endings at the base of the whisker are stimulated. This allows the cat to feel things several inches away from its face. Cats are active in the dark where it is sometimes difficult for them to see, and their whiskers give them another way of finding out about their environment. Because the whiskers extend to the cat's shoulders, some people think they are used to let the cat know how much room it has to move in a tight space. If a cat enters a dark tunnel whose walls brush both the left and right whiskers, that may tell the cat that the tunnel isn't wide enough for it to pass through.

Cats also have a set of whiskers on the insides of each of their front legs above the paws. Some people think these whiskers help the cat catch mice by giving it touch information about the prey animal.

10.

Can cats and dogs see in color?

Yes, but not nearly as well as humans can. Both cats and dogs are red-green color-blind. This means that red objects look dark to these animals, while green objects look white. So when pets look at stoplights, red and green holiday decorations, green trees and red flowers, all they see are different shades of gray.

Cats and dogs can see blue, yellow, and other colors, but, because their eyes have fewer cones (color-sensitive cells) than ours do, they see these colors as pale, washed-out pastels.

11.

Why do cats have retractable claws?

An interesting feature of the cat is its ability to extend its front claws when it wants to scratch, climb, or capture prey. At other times, its claws are pulled back into the paw.

How do cats do this? The cat's claw is attached to a bone in the toe. By flexing its toe (much as we bend our fingers), a cat can retract the claw into the foot. When a cat points its toe, the claw is extended.

One advantage of this arrangement is that the claws are protected while the cat walks, so they stay much sharper. You can see this for yourself, if you have a cat, by comparing the claws on the front feet (which are retractable) with those on the back feet (which are not). The rear claws become dull from wearing against the ground as the cat walks, while the front claws stay needle-sharp.

Retractable claws also help the cat to sneak up on its prey much more quietly. Just think of the difference between a cat's silent walk and the *click-click* of a dog's nonretractable claws as it walks across the floor.

Lions, tigers, and other wild cats all have retractable claws. The only one that doesn't is the cheetah. Like a dog, the cheetah has claws that are extended at all times.

12.
What's the best way to get a cat out of a tree?

At least once in its life, just about every outdoor cat gets "stuck" in a tree. The cat might have been chasing a bird or a squirrel, or simply running away from the neighborhood dog. Whatever the reason, it's now stranded up there, meowing and looking terrified.

What do you do? Many people think they should call the fire department to come to the rescue. But the fire department may actually do more harm than good, for the noise and commotion will probably just scare the cat and drive it even farther up the tree.

The fact is that most cats in trees are surefooted enough to come down by themselves. They just need a little time to think about it and a little help from you.

If your cat is stuck in a tree, here's what to do:
- Look carefully to make sure that it can move around and isn't hurt. (It's not likely that it will be injured, but if it is, you'll need help. Call your local humane society or your veterinarian for advice.)
- Stay calm and quiet. Keep other people and pets away. The last thing a cat wants is a crowd of noisy spectators watching its descent.
- Open a can of its favorite food and place it at the bottom of the tree. Most cats find tuna fish irresistible.
- Now go inside and wait. It may take a few hours, but in almost all cases, your cat will get down the way it went up.

13.

Why are people more allergic to cats than to dogs?

Have you ever been around someone who is allergic to cats? Every time a cat is nearby, the person begins coughing, sneezing, and complaining of a runny nose. Some people are so sensitive that they cannot be in the same house with a cat—even if the animal is in another room. For years, doctors thought it was the cat's fur that made people allergic. They advised their patients not to keep cats as pets, especially long-haired cats.

But then scientists noticed something that didn't make sense. Many of the people who were allergic to cats were *not* allergic to dogs. If the animal's fur were the problem, dogs should bother allergic people just as much as cats do—maybe more, because dogs are bigger and have more hair.

Why should people be more allergic to cats? The answer to this question is very surprising. The thing that makes some people allergic to cats is not the hair at all. It is the cat's saliva.

Cats clean themselves by licking their fur. As they lick, they leave saliva on their coats. Scientists think that the saliva dries and flakes off the cat. When sensitive people breathe in the tiny airborne particles of saliva, they have an allergic reaction. Because all cats lick themselves, short-haired cats can be just as bothersome to allergic people as longhairs.

Dogs, on the other hand, don't lick themselves very much. This may be why people are less likely to have allergies to dogs.

14.

Is it true that cats always land on their feet?

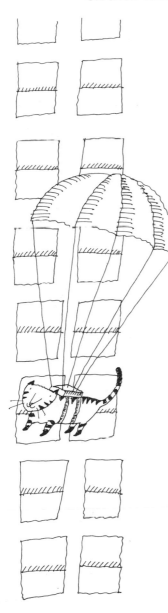

One of the most common beliefs about cats is that a falling cat is always able to land on its feet, even if it falls in an upside-down position. Fortunately for cats, this is usually true. The key to the cat's ability to right itself in midair is its very flexible spine. When a cat finds itself falling, the first thing it does is to twist its back so that its head and front legs are pointing toward the ground. Then it whips its tail over to help turn the rear end of its body right side up. Finally, the cat stretches all four legs out to meet the ground and cushion the shock of landing.

Because cats have this ability, many people think that cats can fall from high places and not get hurt. In fact, some people believe that cats have such good balance that they never fall in the first place.

Unfortunately, this isn't true. Cats do have good balance, but their curiosity sometimes leads them to dangerous places, like roofs or window ledges, where one slip can mean disaster. And landing on all fours doesn't help much when the cat falls from twelve stories up!

Many cat owners don't recognize the danger, and as a result, thousands of cats are hurt or killed each year in falls from open windows or apartment terraces. This kind of accident is so common that veterinarians have a name for it: high-rise syndrome. To protect your pet from high-rise syndrome, make sure all your windows have screens. If you live on a high floor, never leave the windows open even a crack—cats can squeeze through very small spaces—and never let your pet out on a high terrace. Just as with people, an ounce of prevention is worth a pound of cure.

15.
Is there anything special you should do for your pet in the winter?

Yes! You know how miserable winter can be. It's even worse for a pet that has to go outside in the cold and snow. Here are some things you can do to make those freezing days happier for your animal companions.

If you have a cat, keep it indoors during the winter. Cats are small and get chilled very easily. If your cat does go outside, make sure it doesn't stay out too long, and never leave it outside overnight. (Dogs should spend the night inside, too.) If your pet's water bowl is outside, check it often to make sure the water hasn't turned to ice.

Even if you keep your pets indoors, ask your parents to bang on the hood of the car before they start it. Outdoor cats sometimes climb under the hood to sit on the warm motor and can be seriously hurt if they are crouching there when the engine starts.

Unless your dog is paper trained, it will have to go outside for walks in the winter. Try to keep the walks as short as possible. If you have a small or short-haired dog, keep it warm with a dog sweater. When you return from the walk, rinse your dog's feet with fresh water, especially if salt or ice-melting chemicals have been used on the sidewalks. Remember, you may be wearing boots, but your dog (or cat) is going barefoot.

You shouldn't let your dog off its leash at any time, but during the winter it is especially dangerous. Dogs running through the snow can easily lose their sense of direction and become lost because snow covers up most of the smells that dogs use to find their way.

During the winter, your parents may add antifreeze to the car. Antifreeze has a sweet smell that attracts animals, but it is very poisonous to both dogs and cats—as little as one teaspoon can kill an average-size cat. So check underneath the car for puddles and make sure that any spilled antifreeze is cleaned up right away.

16.
How do domestic dogs differ from their wild relatives?

The biggest difference between domestic and wild dogs is, of course, that domestic dogs have been selectively bred over thousands of years to be sociable with humans. Even a tame wolf or coyote can never be trained to live with people as harmoniously as a dog does.

Another important difference is that wild dogs hardly ever bark. While just about all domestic dogs bark (the exception being the basenji, which will bark only if it learns to do so from another dog), wild dogs bark a lot only when they are puppies. By the time they reach adulthood, they are mostly silent.

What is the reason for this odd difference? It is likely that, as humans began to domesticate the dog, they decided that barking was a valuable behavior for dogs to have. A dog who barks is useful as a watchdog and for frightening away intruders. Because they liked this behavior, people may have bred only the dogs who continued to bark as adults. After many years, barking became ingrained as a typical canine behavior.

There are many obvious physical differences between wild and domestic dogs—just compare the body of a wolf with that of a cocker spaniel or a poodle. Features such as curly tails, drooping ears, and pushed-in faces are never seen in wild dogs. These characteristics were selected by humans, who perhaps thought that they made dogs look more cute and cuddly.

A final important difference is the brain size. As the

life of domestic dogs became easier and less challenging, their brains got smaller. In fact, the brain of a wolf may be up to one-fifth larger than the brain of a wolf-size dog.

17.
What are tortoiseshell and calico cats, and what is odd about them?

A tortoiseshell cat is one whose fur is a mottled black and orange color. A calico cat is black and orange with patches of white. The odd fact about both these types of cat is that they are almost always female. Male calico and tortoiseshell cats are very rare. Only one in every three thousand calico cats who lives past kittenhood is a male.

The explanation for this strange occurrence comes from genetics. In the cells of all animals are threadlike structures called chromosomes. Carried on the chromosomes are tiny coded messages known as genes. An animal's genes determine almost everything about it— whether it is male or female, what color its eyes, skin, and hair (or fur) are, and so on.

Chromosomes come in pairs. One of these pairs determines whether the animal will be male or female. Females have two X chromosomes, while males have one X and one Y. In cats, the coded messages for black and orange coat color are carried on the X chromosome, but not on the Y.

A male cat, because he has only one X chromosome, can be either black *or* orange. In order to be black *and* orange, the cat needs two X chromosomes, one carrying the gene for black fur and one carrying the gene for orange fur. Since any animal with two X chromosomes must be a female, all black and orange cats are female. The rare male calico or tortoiseshell cat has three sex chromosomes, two X and one Y.

14

18.

What is unusual about white cats with blue eyes?

Pure white, blue-eyed cats are often deaf. In fact, almost half of all completely white cats suffer from genetic deafness. Only one in one hundred nonwhite cats is genetically deaf. As with calico and tortoiseshell cats, the reason comes from genetics. The same gene that gives a cat its snowy white coat also, in many cases, causes a defect in the cat's inner ear. In these cats, a special structure that normally changes sound vibrations into nerve impulses fails to develop. Without this organ, the cat cannot hear. There is no cure for this type of deafness.

The same gene that causes this condition also affects eye color. Blue-eyed white cats are much more likely to be deaf than white cats with eyes of other colors.

How can you tell if a white kitten will be deaf? There is no foolproof way, but if the kitten has gold or green eyes, or if it has a little patch of dark fur on its forehead (which may fade as the cat grows up), the chances are good that it will have normal hearing.

19.

How can you tell if a cat (or dog) is deaf?

If you have a blue-eyed white cat, that should give you a clue that your pet might be deaf. But even nonwhite cats, as well as dogs, can suffer hearing loss, either genetic, or as a result of head injuries, infections, or just old age.

An animal that cannot hear doesn't act the same as other pets. A deaf cat may never learn to meow. It may sleep a lot and, unlike other cats, will not come running at the sound of the can opener. It will seem lost in its own world, not noticing the things that other pets notice. (Many people, misunderstanding these signs, think the cat

15

is just not very smart. Years may go by before they realize their pet cannot hear!)

If you suspect your pet may be deaf, here are some easy tests you can do to find out. Stand where the animal cannot see you and call its name, clap your hands, or make some other loud noise. A deaf animal will not respond. Next, still standing behind the animal, drop something on the floor. Even if your pet cannot hear, this *will* get a reaction, since deaf animals are especially sensitive to vibrations. Finally, have your pet checked by the veterinarian, who should be able to tell you the cause of your pet's hearing loss, and whether anything can be done to cure it.

If your pet is deaf, you will probably have to make some special allowances—like waking it up for dinner. Also, it's important never to let deaf animals outdoors by themselves, since they are especially vulnerable to unexpected dangers.

20.
Is it a good idea to have your cat declawed?

Everyone who has cats knows that they love to sharpen their claws. Many cat owners, in order to protect their furniture, decide to have their pets declawed. Unfortunately, declawing doesn't do much for the cat. The operation is a painful one, and afterward the cat is left defenseless. It can no longer climb trees, either for fun or to get away from dogs. A declawed cat should never be let outdoors, because it will be unable to fight back if it is attacked by another animal. Declawed cats are also more likely to bite if they feel threatened, and cat owners sometimes find that, after declawing, their cats begin to bite them.

16

A good compromise is to buy a sturdy scratching post and train your cat to use it. You should also trim your pet's claws every couple of weeks. With short claws, your cat will do less damage if it makes a mistake and starts sharpening its nails on the living room furniture.

21.
How do you trim your pet's claws?

Both cats and dogs may sometimes need to have their nails clipped. Because a cat's claws are retractable, they are protected when the cat walks and will become very sharp unless they are trimmed regularly. Dogs do not need nail trimming as often because their claws wear against the ground when they walk.

Nail trimming is easy to do, but it's a job best left to a grown-up. You can help by talking softly to your pet to keep it calm while its claws are cut. (Most animals get very upset around nail-trimming time. In most cases, though, what they really don't like is being restrained.)

The first step is to hold the cat on your lap until it is calm and comfortable. Then, holding one paw, press gently on the top of the foot to extend the claw. Using a pair of clippers made specially for pets, clip off just the curved end of the claw. Don't cut too close, or you may nick the vein that extends into the thick part of the claw. To see where the vein stops, hold the cat's claw up to the light. The pink area is the vein.

If your pet yowls or squirms, you may have to introduce it gradually to having its nails clipped. Start with only one or two claws each day and give your pet a treat as soon as the job is finished. When it learns that there is a reward at the end, your pet will soon learn to tolerate, if not enjoy, its manicure.

22.

Are there any diseases that people can get from dogs?

A disease that can be passed from an animal to a person is called a zoonosis. There are several zoonoses you could get from your dog. But don't get nervous and give away your pets—the likelihood of a person getting an illness from an animal is very small.

Bites are a major way diseases are spread from animals to people. Rabies, for example, is usually spread when an infected animal bites a person or another animal. This is why it is vitally important to have your pets vaccinated against rabies. Aside from actual disease, the bite wound itself can become infected, even if the animal who bit you is healthy. You can avoid these problems by knowing how not to get bitten.

Parasites that people can get from dogs include hookworms and roundworms. If a dog is infected, eggs and larvae will be present in the dog's droppings. When people don't clean up after their dogs, the eggs can get into the soil. To avoid these infections, make sure to clean up after your own dog, and don't go barefoot in areas where dogs are allowed to run free. Equally important is taking your dog to the vet regularly to have the animal checked for worms.

Although both cats and dogs can get cancer, it is not possible for this disease to be passed on to people.

23.

Can people get rabies from animals?

Rabies is a virus that is transmitted from animals to people (or to other animals) through saliva. The most common way of getting rabies is through a bite from a wild animal carrying the disease. Raccoons, foxes, and skunks are the most common carriers of rabies.

One reason rabies is such a feared disease is that it's deadly. Anyone bitten by a rabid animal must immediately receive a series of antirabies shots. Only two people have ever lived through an untreated case of rabies.

A rabid animal is a frightening sight. One effect of rabies is to change the animal's personality so that a friendly animal may become violent and aggressive. At a later stage, the animal's throat muscles become paralyzed, causing the animal to foam at the mouth.

Despite its reputation, rabies is one of the easiest diseases to avoid. Most people never get close enough to a wild animal to be bitten, so the only way you would get rabies is if your dog or cat were bitten and it, in turn, bit you. You can prevent this by having your pet vaccinated against rabies.

24.
How long do dogs and cats live?

Compared to people, dogs and cats don't live very long at all. The average lifespan of a cat is between fourteen and twenty years. Dogs usually live between eight and fifteen years. Where your pet will fall in this range depends on its individual makeup, how healthy it is, and how well you take care of it. Some cat owners have reported pampered felines living into their thirties, but this is the exception rather than the rule.

In dogs, the average lifespan varies from breed to breed. Oddly enough, large breeds, such as Great Danes and Saint Bernards, don't usually live as long as smaller breeds, such as Chihuahuas. Both dogs and cats live longer and healthier lives when they are kept indoors, fed a nutritious diet, and taken to the veterinarian for regular checkups. Pets that have to fend for themselves have a much harder time. In fact, some experts believe that most stray dogs and cats live less than two years.

25.
How do dog years compare to people years?

Although your dog may only live to be fifteen years old, it's a lot older at fifteen than you will be.

It has long been thought that one human year is equal to seven dog years (making a one-year-old dog equivalent to a seven-year-old human). But in reality, it's not that simple.

Dogs do most of their growing up during their first year of life. By age one, a dog is full grown and is able to have puppies. A one-year-old dog is about the same as a fifteen-year-old person. At two, your dog is equivalent to a twenty-four-year-old adult. For each of the next two dog years, add four human years (so a four-year-old dog is the same as a thirty-two-year-old person).

If your dog is over four years old, add five human years for each dog year. When you figure it out this way, dogs and people have almost the same life expectancy. It is easier to understand that a twelve-year-old dog is a senior citizen if you realize that the dog is really seventy-two in human years.

26.
How can you tell how old your pet is?

If you've had your pet since it was a kitten or puppy, it's easy to keep track of how old it is. But when you take in a stray or adopt a grown animal from a shelter, you may have no idea of your pet's age. How can you tell if your new dog or cat is four or fourteen?

The animal's behavior should give you some clues. A canine or feline senior citizen won't be as lively and ener-

20

getic as a younger animal. Also, older pets will probably spend more time asleep.

Like people, pets begin to look different as they age. White hairs around the muzzle are a sure sign that your dog is getting old.

The best way to determine your pet's age, though, is to have a veterinarian look at its teeth. In many animals, including people, the first set of teeth are "baby teeth" that fall out and are replaced by permanent teeth as the animal grows up. By looking at the number of adult teeth a dog or cat has, the veterinarian can accurately pinpoint the age of a young animal.

For dogs and cats that already have all their adult teeth, the veterinarian can estimate the animal's age by seeing how sharp the teeth are. The older the animal is, the more smooth and worn down the teeth will be.

27.
Why don't dogs and cats live as long as people do?

No one understands completely why some animals live longer than others. It is true, though, that the lifespans of different animals vary tremendously. The oldest animal on record is a giant tortoise, which lived for 152 years *after* it was captured as an adult in 1766. The tiny mayfly, on the other hand, has the shortest lifespan of any animal—it lives for just one day.

Scientists have found several factors that influence how long an animal lives. One of these is body size. In general, the bigger an animal is, the longer it lives.

Brain size is important, too. Animals with large brains tend to have longer lifespans than those with small brains.

An animal's metabolism—how hard its body must

work to produce energy—also affects how long it lives. Hamsters, mice, and other small pets have very high metabolisms. Their bodies are constantly in motion, working to produce the energy they need to stay alive. This may help account for their short lifespans—five or six years at most.

Both dogs and cats have smaller bodies, smaller brains, and higher metabolisms than people, so it's no surprise that they don't live as long.

28.
How old should a puppy be to become a pet?

The best time for a puppy to join a human family is when the animal is between eight and twelve weeks old. A puppy should stay with its mother until it is eight weeks old. Part of the reason for this is that a very young puppy may have trouble surviving on its own. Another reason is that, during its first eight weeks, a puppy learns a lot from its mother and its brothers and sisters about what it means to be a dog.

From its mother, the puppy learns some of the rules of good dog behavior. A puppy who acts up is quickly punished with a shake by the scruff of the neck. The puppy also learns that it can get back in its mother's good graces by taking a submissive position (going "belly up").

By playing and play-fighting with the other puppies in the litter, the puppy practices behaviors it will use when it grows up. It also discovers just how hard it can bite without being bitten in return.

If a puppy is taken away from the litter too early, it won't have a chance to learn these valuable lessons. This can mean real trouble when it grows up. Because it won't understand the signals dogs give each other, it will not know how to get out of a dogfight or how to be friends with other dogs.

By eight weeks of age, a puppy has learned the basics of being a dog. Now it is time for it to learn to live with people. Between the ages of eight and twelve weeks is the easiest time for a dog to learn this. If a dog does not have loving contact with people during this time, it may never be very friendly with people and it may never make a good pet.

29.
Is it possible for a wolf and a dog to reproduce together?

Yes. Although wolves and dogs are different species, they are closely related—enough so that they can mate. Dogs and coyotes can also interbreed.

Some people like the idea of having a wolf-dog as a pet. But because of the wild animal in them, it is impossible to predict how these hybrids will act. Some wolf-dogs grow up to have good temperaments, but many others turn into fearful, unpredictable (and dangerous) animals. They can also be very aggressive and are nearly impossible to train.

If you like the look of a wolf-dog, a better idea is to get a breed of dog that resembles a wolf, but has a good disposition and can be trained. Such breeds include the German shepherd, the husky, and the Alaskan malamute.

30.
What is there around the house that could be poisonous to dogs and cats?

When people think of household poisons, they usually list insecticides and cleaning products—things that are equally dangerous to people and animals. You might be surprised at how many things around your house are safe for you but hazardous for your pet.

Many people don't know, for instance, that aspirin is poisonous to cats. Even fewer people realize that dogs can have a bad reaction to chocolate. Chocolate contains a substance called theobromine, which is toxic to dogs. As little as one chocolate bar can make an average-size dog very sick.

Other things around your house would be poisonous to you if you ate them, although it's not very likely that you would. Your pet, though, doesn't always know better. Both cats and dogs can die from licking car antifreeze. Antifreeze is especially dangerous because its sweet smell makes it attractive to animals.

Some of the plants around your house could be dangerous to both you and your pet. You probably don't have the habit of chewing on your plants, but your cat might. Many cats, for reasons no one really understands, love to eat houseplants. If your cat is a plant-eater, you should know which plants are harmful to cats.

Chrysanthemums, Boston ivy, and philodendrons will not kill cats, but they do contain chemicals that cause a painful rash or swelling on their mouths. Plants that make cats sick include asparagus ferns, daffodils, and English ivy. If your cat has eaten any of these plants, it may throw up or seem very ill. You should try to identify which plant it ate and call your veterinarian as soon a possible. Ask your vet or your local humane society for a complete list of poisonous houseplants.

If you find that you do have some poisonous plants in your house, either get rid of them or keep them out of your cat's reach. You can also grow a container of catnip or "kitty herbs" for your cat to nibble, so that it can satisfy its craving on a plant that won't hurt it.

24

31.

How old is a puppy when its eyes open?

You may be surprised to learn that dogs, who depend so much on sight, hearing, and smell as adults, are born without the use of any of these senses. A newborn puppy cannot see or hear, and it can probably smell very little. In fact, besides feeling pain, about the only thing a newborn puppy notices is the difference between warm and cold. A pup stays close to its mother not by seeing, hearing, or smelling her, but by heading toward the warmth of her body. If a puppy is taken away from its mother, it will crawl around blindly until it finds her, or something warm, to snuggle up to.

At about ten to fifteen days, the puppy's eyes open and its senses of hearing and smell start to develop. During the next few weeks its senses develop very quickly. By four weeks of age, a puppy's vision is nearly as good as that of an adult dog.

32.

Do dogs and cats have the same sense of taste as humans?

Like humans, dogs and cats are sensitive to different tastes on different areas of their tongues.

People have four types of taste buds, those sensitive to sour, salty, sweet, and bitter tastes. People taste sour food along the sides of their tongue. Salty foods are tasted along the sides and at the tip of the tongue. Sweet tastes are detected by taste buds at the tip of the tongue, and taste buds sensitive to bitter substances are found at the back of the tongue.

In dogs, the distribution of taste buds is about the same as in people. Dogs, however, taste sweets along the sides and at the tip of the tongue, rather than just at the tip. This may explain why dogs love sweets as much as, or

25

even more than, people do. Dogs also have special taste buds at the tip of the tongue that are sensitive to the taste of water.

If you have a cat, you may have noticed that it doesn't share the "sweet tooth" of both people and dogs. This is because cats do not have taste buds that respond to sweets. Like dogs, however, cats are very sensitive to the taste of water.

33.
Why are some cats born without tails?

For a particular breed of cat, the Manx, not having a tail is its most important feature. Manx cats have been around for nearly five hundred years. The breed comes from the Isle of Man, a small island just off the west coast of England.

There are some fantastic legends to explain how the Manx cat lost its tail. Some people say that when Irish soldiers invaded the Isle of Man they cut off the tails of the island's cats to keep as trophies. Others believe that the Manx is a cross between a cat and a rabbit (even though such a match is not possible). In reality, the Manx has no tail because of a genetic mutation.

Not all Manx cats are tailless. They can have a short stump of a tail or even a full-length tail. Cats with no tail at all are called "rumpies." Those with a short tail are called "stumpies," while those with a complete tail are known as "longies."

The gene that gives the Manx cat no tail also gives it a shorter spine and longer hind legs than other cats. This causes Manx cats to walk with a little hop. With its long back legs, hopping gait, and no tail, it's easy to see how some people think the Manx is part rabbit.

34.

How can dogs hear dog whistles?

Dogs are able to hear much higher pitched sounds than people can. The highest sound an adult human can hear is about 20,000 vibrations per second. Dogs can easily hear frequencies up to 40,000 vibrations per second. Dog whistles make sounds that are within the range of a dog's hearing, but much too high for most people to hear. The exception is very young children, who have more sensitive hearing than adults. Because of this, kids can sometimes hear dog whistles. As they grow up, though, their eardrums get thicker and they lose the ability to hear very high notes.

Both dogs and cats can hear higher pitched sounds than people can. They can also hear very soft sounds better than we can because they have the ability to prick up their ears and to turn their ears toward the source of a sound. Dogs have seventeen separate muscles that let them move their ears up and down and in a wide arc. It's not unusual to see a dog or cat with one ear pointed forward and the other pointed sideways, listening to two different sounds at the same time.

People have nine muscles for moving their ears, but in most people (except for those who can wiggle their ears) none of these muscles work.

35.

Do cats and dogs have a "sixth sense"?

Both cats and dogs possess a unique sense organ that people lack. It is called the vomeronasal organ and is located in the roof of the mouth. Two small openings just behind the front teeth connect the vomeronasal organ to the outside air. To activate this sense, the animal sucks air into its mouth. Scientists know that the vomeronasal system is related to the sense of smell. They think that cats and dogs may use this system in mating to get special chemical information about animals of the opposite sex.

You can tell when your pet is using its vomeronasal sense by watching its behavior. It is especially easy to spot when a cat is using it because the cat shows an odd behavior called "flehmen." During flehmen, the cat opens its mouth slightly, pulls back its lips, and inhales, drawing scent molecules up into the openings leading to the vomeronasal organ. Flehmen means "grimace" in German, and a cat doing this does look as though it is grimacing with disgust.

36.
What should you do if you have to get rid of your pet?

The best solution is not to get a pet if you are not sure you'll be able to care for it all its life. Before you get a pet, find out the average lifespan of the animal you are interested in. Then figure out how old you will be when your pet is an adult. If you are twelve years old and you want to get a puppy, will you still want a dog when you are in your twenties? If you are not sure, think twice about adopting or buying a pet.

Sometimes, though, even responsible pet owners have to get rid of a pet. The best thing for you to do is to find your pet a new home. Remember that the older your pet is, the more difficult it will be for it to adjust to a new family. If your pet is not well trained, you'll have a harder time finding someone to take it. Don't give away a pet because it has a bad habit, such as chewing or wetting in the house. If you don't want it because of its bad behavior, no one else will either. Instead of giving away a problem pet, call your local humane society for advice on how to solve your pet's behavior problem.

If you have really tried and you still can't find a good home for your pet, you can always bring it to an animal shelter where it has a chance of being adopted. But don't expect miracles. Even if every person in the United States adopted a dog or cat, there would still not be enough good homes for all the animals in shelters.

Whatever you do, *don't* get rid of your pet by abandoning it on the street to fend for itself. Dogs and cats are not as independent as people think they are. The dangers of disease, traffic, and other animals cut a stray pet's life expectancy down to only two years.

37.
What should you do if your pet gets lost?

If your pet gets lost, you have to act fast. The sooner you begin looking for it, the better your chances will be that it's still nearby.

Call and visit the lost and found department of your local animal shelter to find out if your pet has been turned in. It will help if you can give the shelter a full description of the animal, including breed, sex, color, markings, age, size, and anything else that makes your pet special.

Draw a lost pet poster, including a photograph of your pet, if you have one. Offer a reward and put down a phone number where you or someone else can be reached at all hours. Make enough copies of the poster so that you can put one on every street corner at least six blocks in all directions from where your pet was lost.

Ask your parents to place an ad in the lost and found section of your local newspaper. Finally, be patient and keep looking. Lost pets sometimes show up weeks or months later.

Of course, the best thing to do is not to lose your pet in the first place. To keep your dog from getting lost, make sure it always wears its license and ID tag. Keep it on a leash and never tie it up outside or leave it alone outside your home.

If you have a cat, make sure all your windows have screens and don't let your pet run loose outside. Get an elastic cat collar with an ID tag, and be sure your cat wears it.

Having your pet spayed or neutered will also help, because it will be less likely to wander away from home.

38.
Is it okay to feed your cat dog food (and vice versa)?

Dogs and cats are different species and need very different kinds of food. For their small size, cats need a lot of protein, particularly meat, fish, or fowl. In fact, cats have to eat more protein every day than either dogs or humans in order to stay healthy. Unlike dogs and people, cats cannot become vegetarians.

Most dog food probably doesn't have enough protein, or enough of the right kind of protein, for your cat. It also doesn't contain enough taurine, something that dogs do not need but that cats need for good vision.

An occasional meal of dog food or people food will not hurt your cat, and cat food once in a while isn't too bad for your dog. But for most of its meals your pet should eat a food designed for its special needs.

39.
Why do people think that black cats bring bad luck?

The belief that black cats are bad luck almost certainly started in the Middle Ages, when cats were associated with witchcraft and black magic. During the fourteenth cen-

tury, it was thought that witches kept animal companions, called familiars, to carry out their evil work. Some people thought that witches could actually turn themselves into cats. These ideas probably got started because of the cat's air of mystery, its cunning, and its habit of being active at night. Black cats may have seemed especially dangerous because they are so hard to see in the dark.

These beliefs made the Middle Ages a bad time for cats. When witches were tried, their cats were often tried (and executed) along with them. It was also common to sacrifice cats in order to rid a town of evil spirits. The superstition about a black cat crossing one's path came from a belief that the cat was marking a path to the devil.

Luckily, people realized after a time that cats could help in controlling disease by catching rats. Once the cat's worth was understood, people began to treat cats with more respect. However, some of the old superstitions about cats have carried over to the present day.

40.
What breed of dog can run the fastest?

The fastest dog is the saluki, which has been clocked at over forty miles per hour. The saluki is also believed to be the world's oldest purebred dog. It was originally bred at least nine thousand years ago by Arab tribesmen for the purpose of hunting antelopes, gazelles, and other swift prey. Salukis are part of a group of dogs known as gazehounds. Unlike dogs that rely on their sense of smell, gazehounds use their very sharp vision to chase down game. Their lightweight bodies allow them to run as fast as the animals they pursue.

The saluki gets its name from the ancient Arabian city of Saluk. Even today, salukis and their relatives, the

Afghan hounds, are used in the Middle East to hunt antelopes and gazelles.

41.

Why do some dogs have long, pointed noses while others have short, flat noses?

Dogs use their noses not only for smelling things, but also to cool themselves off. The inside of a dog's nose is a maze of moisture-covered surfaces. When the dog pants, it breathes in cool air through its nose. The air flows over the moist surfaces and cools them by evaporation. A dog has very few sweat glands, so its entire cooling system works through its nose.

Dogs who work hard or run long distances need bigger and more effective cooling systems than dogs who sit quietly most of the time. It is no accident that dogs bred for running, racing, and chasing prey have some of the longest noses in the dog world. Some long-nosed breeds are the greyhound, the whippet, the deerhound, and the saluki. All of these dogs are very strong and fast runners.

Dogs bred to be house pets, on the other hand, are not expected to be very active. They can get by with smaller cooling systems. The Pekingese, with its flat, pushed-in face, is a good example of this type of dog.

42.

Why do animals have tails?

One way that humans differ from other animals is that almost all animals have tails. Tails come in a range of sizes and have a wide variety of uses.

In some animals, such as the kangaroo, the tail is very large and is used for both balance and support. Some monkeys use their tails almost like an extra hand for grasping things and hanging from tree branches. Fish depend on their feathery tail fins to move them through the water. And in cows and horses, the tail serves as a very effective flyswatter!

In dogs and cats, the tail has another important function—it tells us how the animal is feeling. Dogs wag their tails when they are happy and put them between their legs when they've done something wrong. And anyone who's seen an angry cat with its tail puffed out like a brush knows that cats talk with their tails as well.

TWO Birds, Fish, and Other Creatures

43.
Can having a pet fish make you feel better?

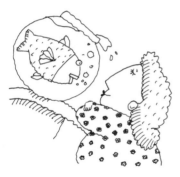

Watching fish can actually be as relaxing as being hypnotized! When scientists studied patients waiting in a dentist's office, they found that the patients looking at a tank of fish were calm, while those who looked at an empty tank remained nervous and fearful about seeing the dentist. Hypnosis is sometimes used to relax patients in situations like this, but the fish proved to be just as effective.

For people who want the calming effect that fish can give, but don't want the responsibility of a pet, there is a company that makes "fish tank" videotapes. Just pop one into your video machine and enjoy an hour of watery relaxation.

44.
What is unusual about the teeth of rabbits and guinea pigs?

They never stop growing! Unlike the teeth of humans and most other animals, which grow to a certain length and then stop, guinea pig and rabbit teeth grow continually—much as our fingernails do. In the wild, the teeth are worn down as the animal gnaws on wood and other hard objects. When kept as pets, however, rabbits and guinea pigs may be fed soft foods that do not allow them to wear down their teeth. The result can be teeth that grow so long that the animal can no longer eat properly or even close its mouth. It is important, if you have one of these animals as a pet, to give it hard foods such as raw carrots and brussels sprouts, along with a block of wood to gnaw on.

Other animals whose teeth continue to grow throughout life are walruses, elephants, and wild boars.

45.
Do animals such as wolves and wild cats make good pets?

No! But it's easy to see why people want them. For one thing, it seems much more exciting to have a lion cub or an ocelot as a pet than a plain old house cat. Also, stories about people who have tamed and made friends with wild animals make us think that, if we treat them kindly, wild animal babies will grow up to be gentle and tame around humans.

Unfortunately, it doesn't usually work out that way. It is true that many wild animals, such as raccoons and even lions and wolves, are playful and cute when they are young. Because they are small and uncoordinated, they aren't very dangerous. Many wild babies seem very friendly with people and will even drink from a baby bottle. But the young animal isn't really being friendly. It is just acting as if the human caretaker were its mother. As the wild baby grows up, it relies less and less on its mother and begins to act more wild. As its teeth and claws get bigger, it also becomes dangerous to people. This is why most people who adopt an orphaned wild animal or buy an exotic pet find that they must give the animal away when it grows up.

Another reason not to have a wild pet is that you can never give the animal as good a home as it would have in nature. Lions in the wild, for example, roam large territories, hunting at night and sleeping during the day. You can imagine how unhappy a lion would be if it were confined to a small house and fed canned cat food. Unlike a domestic cat, a lion can't learn to adapt its habits to life with people.

So, if you're dreaming of having a pet wolf or lion, do yourself and the animal a favor and choose a dog or cat instead. Watch your dog as it marks its territory and your cat as it stalks and pounces on a catnip mouse. If you observe their behaviors carefully, you'll see the wolf in your dog and the lion in your cat, and you'll find that a domestic pet can be every bit as fascinating as a wild one.

46.
Is it possible to train a goldfish to do tricks?

It's possible to train almost any animal to do something. Many people think that fish are not smart enough to learn tricks, but that just isn't true.

Because a fish is confined in an aquarium, the number of things it can learn is limited—obviously you'll never be able to train your fish to walk on a leash, but that isn't because it is stupid! Choosing a behavior your fish can do is the first key to success. The second key is to be patient. Some animals are faster learners than others, so don't expect your fish to learn a new trick in one day.

A simple trick you can teach your fish is to come to the top of the tank in response to a signal from you. A good signal to use is a tap on the side of the fish tank.

Fish naturally swim to the top of the tank when they are fed. So each time you feed your fish, first tap lightly on the side of the tank. Then immediately sprinkle fish food onto the water. You may have to repeat the "tap-food" training for several weeks to see any results. Make certain that you don't train your fish so much that you overfeed them.

After a while you'll begin to notice that the fish swim to the top of the tank whenever you tap on the side. The tap has become a signal that they are about to be fed. You can teach them to respond to any other signal you choose, provided the fish can detect it. Turning the lights on and off a few times is another good signal to use.

47.
How do fish breathe?

Like people and all other living things, fish have to breathe in order to stay alive. But how is it possible for them to breathe underwater?

Surprisingly, fish and people breathe in basically the same way: by taking in *oxygen* and expelling *carbon dioxide*. People take their oxygen from the air, while fish get dissolved oxygen from the water. When a fish breathes, it sucks water into its mouth and forces the water over its gills. The gills take oxygen from the water and expel carbon dioxide. The "used" water flows out through the gill covers, which are found just behind the fish's cheeks.

48.
How can you tell what size tank your goldfish need?

The first thing to think about when picking out a tank is not whether the fish will have enough room to swim, but whether they will have room to breathe.

As you know, fish breathe by taking dissolved oxygen from the water. What happens when the fish use up all the oxygen in the water? The fact that aquarium fish don't die tells us that oxygen must have a way of getting back into the water so there will be a constant supply for the fish to

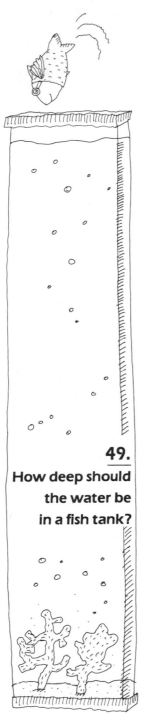

breathe. The place where this happens is the water's surface. Here oxygen from the air is absorbed into the water and the extra carbon dioxide in the water goes back into the air.

To get enough oxygen to survive, each fish in a tank needs a certain amount of water surface area. A good rule is to allow 24 square inches of water surface for every inch of fish. So if you have five 2-inch fish (10 inches total), they will need 240 square inches of water surface. That means a tank at least 24 inches long and 10 inches wide.

In addition to giving them a big enough tank, you can do some other things to help your fish breathe more easily:
· Get an air stone. These porous stones blow a stream of air bubbles into the tank and circulate the water. This helps the water to absorb oxygen.
· Put some underwater plants in the tank. In a process called photosynthesis, plants use up carbon dioxide and produce oxygen—exactly what the fish need.

49.
How deep should the water be in a fish tank?

A deeper tank will give your fish more room to swim around, so they will probably be happier in a deep tank than in a shallow one. But remember—just because your tank is deep doesn't mean that you can put more fish in it. A 24-inch by 12-inch tank filled with 12 inches of water will not hold any more fish than the same tank filled with 8 inches of water.

Another important thing to think about is weight. Fish tanks full of water can be surprisingly heavy. A 24- by 12-inch tank filled with 12 inches of water weighs in at 120 pounds! If the water is 15 inches deep, the weight goes up to 150 pounds.

50.

How can you tell if your goldfish is male or female?

It is usually very difficult to tell, as the only time male and female goldfish look different from one another is when they are ready to breed. At that time, the male develops small white spots, known as tubercles, on his gill covers (just behind the cheeks). Don't confuse this with "white spot disease," in which small white spots appear all over the fish's body.

The female in breeding condition will fill up with eggs and look fatter than the male. If you have two males or two females, they will probably never come into breeding condition, so you might never learn what sex they are.

51.

Why do horses need shoes?

A horse's hoof is a complicated structure. Made out of a hard, hornlike material, it's specially designed to carry up to several thousand pounds (the weight of a full-grown horse).

A horse's hoof continues to grow throughout its lifetime. The hoof grows about one-third of an inch per month. In the wild, horses' hooves wear down to compensate for that growth.

Domestic horses, however, have to walk on a variety of surfaces and do many different jobs. Because of this, their hooves need special protection. Horses that walk on pavement or other hard roads and horses that carry heavy loads need shoes to keep their hooves from wearing down too much. The shoe is made of a curved piece of metal that is nailed onto the bottom of the hoof. Because the hoof keeps growing, a horse may need to have its shoes changed or adjusted every few months.

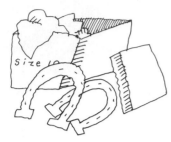

There are many different types of horseshoes designed for the various kinds of work a horse does. Draft horses wear thick iron shoes to withstand the wear of city streets. These shoes are sometimes padded with leather or rubber to soften the shock, and spikes can be added to give the horse better footing in ice and snow. Racehorses wear lightweight aluminum shoes for greater speed. Most racehorses get a new pair of shoes before each race.

Horses that walk on very soft ground may not need shoes at all. In fact, these horses sometimes must have their hooves trimmed to keep them from growing too long—just as we trim our fingernails.

52.
Do horses really sleep standing up?

Horses spend about eight hours of every day asleep, and for most of that time they doze standing up. Standing is the safest way for a horse to sleep—if danger threatens, the animal wakes up quickly and is already on its feet and ready to run. When a horse feels it is in danger, it may never lie down to sleep, since lying down is a vulnerable position.

Scientists have found, however, that a horse can only go into deep sleep and dream when it is lying down. A horse in deep sleep lies on its side with all four legs sticking out. Deep sleep usually takes place for a couple of hours during the night, which is why most people never see it. It is difficult to awaken a horse from a deep sleep. Some observers of wild horses have reported that when a herd comes to rest one or two lookouts always remain standing to alert the others in case of danger.

53.

Why doesn't a sleeping bird fall off its perch?

If you have a parakeet, finch, or another type of bird as a pet, you may have wondered how it can sleep while sitting on its perch. Actually, the more deeply the bird sleeps, the *less* likely it is to fall. The grip of a bird's claws is controlled by a long tendon that runs around the back of the bird's leg. The more the tendon stretches, the tighter the claws grip. As the bird relaxes into deep sleep, it settles down onto the perch, bending its leg joints. As the leg joints bend, the tendon to the claws begins to stretch and the bird's hold on its perch gets tighter.

54.

Do mice make good pets?

Although you might not think so, mice are friendly and can make very good pets, especially if you take the time to tame them and play with them. Mice and their relatives, hamsters and gerbils, are a good choice if you live in an apartment building that does not allow dogs or cats.

Even though mice are tiny, they do need responsible care and lots of attention. Before you get a mouse as a pet, ask yourself these questions:

• Does everyone in the family like the idea of having a mouse as a pet? If anyone is afraid of or dislikes mice, getting one isn't fair to that person, or to the animal.

• Are you prepared to take care of your mouse, including trips to the veterinarian, if necessary, for as long as it lives? (Mice usually live about three years.)

• Will you remember that a mouse is much smaller than you and needs to be handled gently?

• Can you afford to buy a cage, complete with exercise wheel, bedding, water bottle, and other things your mouse needs?

• Do you have at least an hour a day to take care of your mouse and play with it?

If you answer yes to all these questions, then a mouse may be right for you.

The place to start is a good pet shop, where you should be able to buy a mouse, as well as the cage, other equipment, and a book on mouse care. (The best thing you can buy for any kind of pet is a good book on how to take care of it.)

Once you get your new pet home, it will need a few days to adjust to its surroundings. During this time, you may approach the cage quietly and put your hand inside so the mouse gets used to the way you smell. Be still and let the mouse come to you.

When the mouse approaches you without fear, you can begin taming it by offering it a small food treat between your fingers. Before too long, your mouse will learn to eat out of your hand and do simple tricks for a food reward. You should gently handle and play with your mouse every day. The more time you spend with it, the friendlier and tamer a pet it will be.

55.
How can you tell if your bird is sick?

Like other animals, birds sometimes get sick. But unlike many other animals, birds don't usually act as sick as they are. One reason may be that a bird's natural instinct for survival prevents it from showing any sign of weakness that would make it easy prey for a larger animal. If a bird looks healthy and strong, there is more chance that a potential predator will leave it alone. So most birds pretend to be healthy even when they're not.

Because of this trait, bird owners need to be very

observant. When a bird begins to look sick, it is probably already quite ill. If you have a bird, watch it closely every day for any of these early warning signs: changes in behavior or appearance—such as more sleeping, less talking or singing, sitting with feathers fluffed up—or changes in eating habits. If your bird shows any of these signs, it's time to call the veterinarian.

56.
What kinds of birds can be taught to talk?

The best talkers in the bird world are parrots, lovebirds, parakeets, and other *hookbill* birds. This group of birds can be recognized by their short curved beaks, thick tongues, and claws that are used for climbing and grasping, much as we use our hands. Just about all hookbill birds have an uncanny ability to imitate human speech, learning not just words and phrases, but also the different tones of voice of different people.

When a bird learns to talk, it does not think about what it says. It simply learns to repeat what it has heard people say. It is not true, however, that a talking bird will repeat anything that is said to it. Training a bird to talk takes great patience. You must be willing to work with your bird every day, repeating the word or phrase you want it to learn over and over again. Once the word has been learned, you will probably have to repeat it from time to time so that the bird does not forget.

The world's best talking bird is reputed to be the African gray parrot, a light gray bird with a brilliant red tail. There are stories of African grays that have learned dozens of different words. But you don't need such an exotic pet to get a talker. Even the common parakeet can be taught to speak and do tricks if you have the patience.

43

57.
Why do birds need to eat gravel?

Gravel, sometimes also called health grit, is necessary for a seed-eating bird to digest its food. Since birds do not have teeth and therefore cannot chew their food, they must swallow seeds whole. When the seeds reach the bird's gizzard (the same thing as our stomach), they must be broken up in order to be digested. This is where the gravel comes in. The gravel a bird swallows stays in its gizzard and helps to grind up the seeds the bird has eaten.

The type of gravel a bird needs depends on the bird's size. Finches, parakeets, canaries, and other small birds need fine gravel, while larger birds such as parrots need much coarser gravel. The gravel remains in the gizzard for a long time, so it is important not to feed your bird too much. Some bird experts say you should give no more than a small pinch of grit once or twice a week. Your veterinarian should be able to tell you what is right for your bird.

58.
Do hamsters make good pets?

Hamsters, like mice, make great pets and are easy to care for. They are a good choice if you want a pet but cannot have a dog or cat.

The breed most commonly kept as a pet is the golden hamster, which was brought to this country from Syria in the 1930s. In the wild, the golden hamster lives in burrows in the earth that are up to eight feet deep. The name hamster comes from the German word *hamstern*, which means "to hoard." The hamster earned its name because of its distinctive habit of storing extra food in its cheek pouches and hiding food in the corners of its cage.

Hamsters do not get along very well with each other,

so it is better to keep just one as a pet. Two hamsters, even if they are of the same sex, may fight bitterly. If you have two hamsters of the opposite sex and you are not careful to keep them apart, you'll almost certainly end up with lots of babies—in theory, these animals can produce as many as twenty litters of pups in one year.

Hamsters eat grains, mouse pellets, fruits, and vegetables. Like other rodents, hamsters have teeth that grow continually, so they'll also need a block of wood to chew on.

Hamsters are very active. Because they are nocturnal, they prefer to exercise at night and sleep during the day. Make sure to give your pet an exercise wheel in its cage. You can also take it out of the cage to exercise and explore if you watch it closely.

59.
How are hamsters different from gerbils?

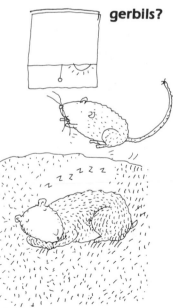

Both these small rodents make good pets, but they differ in several important ways. While hamsters have been kept as pets in this country since the 1930s, gerbils have only been popular as pets for the last ten to fifteen years. The first gerbils were brought to the United States in 1954, not as pets, but to be used in scientific experiments.

Unlike hamsters, which don't get along well with each other, gerbils are very sociable. And while hamsters prefer to sleep during the day and play at night, gerbils, like people, do just the opposite.

How do you decide between a hamster and a gerbil as a pet? If you have the time or money to care for only one animal, a hamster is a better choice, since these animals like to live alone. Gerbils, on the other hand, should be kept in pairs or groups, because they become very lonely by themselves.

If you want a pet that is active when you are awake, get gerbils. Hamsters, because they are nocturnal, will tend to be quiet during the day.

Aside from these differences, hamsters and gerbils are quite similar. Both need daily exercise and will become more tame and friendly the more they are handled.

60.
**How can you tell
if your bird
is male or female?**

It all depends on what kind of bird you have. In some species it is very easy to distinguish males from females just by looking at them. The most striking example of a male-female difference is in the peacock. Only male peacocks have the familiar, brilliantly colored tail feathers. Females (called peahens) are smaller, gray, somewhat dowdy-looking birds.

Among some other birds, males and females look so much alike that even bird experts have a hard time telling the difference. In many species of parrots, for example, both sexes are brightly colored. Male and female parrots act pretty much the same and, in the talking species, both can be taught to talk equally well. In these cases, the only way to tell male from female is for a veterinarian to make a small cut in the bird's abdomen and look inside with a tool called an endoscope. Though this procedure is not dangerous to the bird, it is usually not worth doing. Since many males and females look and act the same, most bird owners don't really care what sex their pet is.

If you have a parakeet, you can tell male from female by looking at the bare skin around the bird's nostrils. On a male, this area is bright blue, while on a female it is brown, pink, or tan.

You can determine the sex of your canary, not by the

way it looks, but by the way it acts. Only male canaries sing, so if yours is silent, you probably have a female.

61.
Why do ferrets smell so bad?

Ferrets, which are sometimes kept as pets, are members of the family *Mustelidae*. Other animals in this group are weasels, minks, badgers, and skunks.

Though these animals look very different from one another, they all share a common characteristic—the ability to give off a strong, musky odor when they are excited or disturbed.

The animal most famous for this behavior is, of course, the skunk, which is able to spray its scent directly at the animal or person that's bothering it. Other mustelids haven't developed this talent, but they do produce a very strong smell when they are alarmed. It is obvious that the ferret's strong smell is useful in getting rid of other animals that might like to prey on it. The odor may also be used as a kind of chemical signal between ferrets.

62.
Do ferrets make good pets?

Although they are related to weasels and skunks, ferrets are considered by some people to be domestic animals. They do have a long association with people. Ferrets have been raised in captivity since Roman times. They were first imported to the United States in the 1800s.

Ferrets are excellent hunters. One ferret can easily keep an entire household free of rats and mice. In fact, it was probably this skill that led people to keep ferrets in the first place.

Ferrets are intelligent animals. Like dogs and cats,

they can usually be trained to walk on a leash and use a litter pan. Unlike dogs and cats, however, ferrets can be very unpredictable. When frightened, a ferret is likely to bite, and its sharp teeth can inflict a serious wound.

Another drawback to keeping ferrets as pets is their strong, musky smell. Both males and females give off this odor, especially when they are excited or upset.

Like weasels and minks, ferrets have a great deal of energy and spend much of their time running around. Since they are naturally nocturnal, most of this activity takes place at night.

If you're still interested in having a pet ferret, check your local laws. In many places, ferrets are classified as wild animals and are illegal to own.

63.

Do snakes and lizards really have a "third eye"?

Yes. Many reptiles, and some fish, do have an actual third eye located in the center of their foreheads and covered by skin or scales. This eye does not see images as our eyes do, but is sensitive to light and to the angle of the sun's rays.

When the sun is directly overhead, the light shines straight down on the third eye and lets the animal know it is noontime. When the sun is low, its rays strike the third eye at an angle, telling the animal it is dawn or dusk.

People see the angle of the sun through their regular eyes, but this information isn't terribly important to them. Why is it so important to reptiles that they have a special eye to detect it?

Knowing the time of day is vital for cold-blooded animals, which use the sun's warmth to regulate their body temperature. When the third eye sees light at an angle, this helps tell the reptile that it is morning: time to come out to bask in the sun and begin warming up. The noon sun blazing down alerts the lizard, through its third eye, that it is in danger of overheating and should seek out some shade. Scientists found out about the third eye's function by covering it up and seeing how the animal behaved. When a lizard had its third eye covered with foil, it spent the whole day in the sun, not seeming to know when to look for some shade.

A lizard whose third eye has been covered has more trouble finding its way back when it is removed from its home territory. This tells us that these animals also use the angle of the sun's rays as a kind of signpost to help them get around in their environment.

64.
Why does a snake shed its skin?

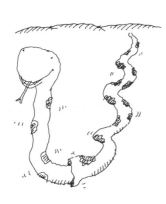

For snakes, shedding is a way to get rid of skin that has become worn out or too small. People also shed their worn skin, but they do it continually, and the old skin flakes off in tiny pieces, rather than all at once. In fact, most people are only aware of shedding when their skin peels after a bad sunburn.

A snake's skin is not very elastic—that is, it cannot stretch as the animal grows. Because of this, a growing snake must shed its skin frequently and replace it with new, larger skin. Baby snakes shed for the first time very soon after they are born. In a snake's first year of life, it may shed as many as seven times. Once a snake reaches its full size, it does not shed as often. When it does, it is usually to replace a worn-out skin, rather than to escape one that has been outgrown.

You can tell when a snake is getting ready to shed by watching the color of its skin. As the old skin pulls away from the new layer underneath, it takes on a cloudy, whitish color. The snake does not move around much at this stage, partly because it cannot see very well through the layer of dead skin covering its eyes.

Shedding usually begins with the snake yawning and rubbing its nose on the ground. Both these actions loosen the old skin around the snake's mouth and help to push the skin back. After this, the snake literally crawls out of its old skin, which is turned completely inside out. The whole shedding process can take as little as a few minutes or as long as several days.

65.
How can you tell a land turtle from a water turtle?

Although at first glance all turtles look pretty much alike, they actually have different body shapes especially adapted to the place where they live. Once you know what to look for, it's easy to tell the difference.

In water turtles, the top part of the shell (called the carapace) is flattened and streamlined. This allows the turtle to slip easily through the water. Webbed feet help the water turtle to be a good swimmer.

Water turtles do, indeed, spend most of their time in the water. In fact, some water turtles cannot even swallow their food unless their heads are submerged. About the only time they come out of the water is to sit on a rock or log and bask in the sun.

Turtles that live mainly on land are usually called tortoises. Unlike water turtles, tortoises have high, domed carapaces. Their legs are short and stumpy, like tiny elephants—not at all suited for swimming. Tortoises do not swim well and can easily drown if they get into water deeper than their shell. Tortoises are often found in dry deserts where a water turtle would never survive.

66.

How can you tell a male turtle from a female turtle?

In most species of turtle and tortoise, you can tell male from female by looking at the tail. Males usually have a thicker, longer tail than females. In addition, male water turtles have longer claws on their front feet. Female water turtles are often bigger in overall size, however.

Tortoises also differ in the size of the tail, with the male having a longer tail. Among male tortoises, the bottom shell is somewhat concave.

For some species, the differences between male and female are most obvious during the breeding season. All year long, male box turtles have eyes that are somewhat red. During breeding season this color becomes much more intense, making the male look as though he has a bright red eye. So when it is most important for box turtles to tell the difference between boy and girl, it is easiest for them to do so.

67.

Are rabbits members of the rodent family?

No. Although rabbits seem very similar to guinea pigs, hamsters, and other rodents, they are actually quite different. Rabbits are classified as *Lagomorpha*, a small order of mammals including only rabbits, hares, and pikas. Lagomorphs all have long ears, short, upturned tails, and long hind legs that give them their peculiar hopping gait. Unlike rodents, rabbits do not use their front feet to pick up pieces of food.

There are differences even among lagomorphs. Baby rabbits are born naked, while baby hares are born with all their fur. And there are no domesticated hares, so if you have a pet bunny, you can be certain it is a rabbit.

68.

Why do rabbits have such big ears?

The most striking feature of rabbits and hares is certainly their long ears. In wild rabbits, the ears are usually three to four inches long. In lop-eared rabbits, which are selectively bred to have large, drooping ears, the ears can measure up to fourteen inches in length.

Rabbits that live in the wild have many natural enemies, including wolves, coyotes, and wildcats. Rabbits aren't fast enough to outrun most of these predators, so they must be able to hear them coming while there is still time to get away. To survive, the rabbit needs a good sense of hearing. Like a dog, the rabbit can prick up its ears and turn them in the direction of a sound. The size of the ears is also important—because they are so big, the ears act as funnels for sound, allowing the rabbit to hear even the faintest noises. To see what it's like to have such sensitive hearing, cup your hands behind your ears. You'll notice that everything sounds much louder.

69.

Do animals ever have pets?

There have been many stories about different kinds of animals being friends, but the first animal who actually had a pet was a "talking" gorilla named Koko. For over ten years, Koko, a 230-pound female gorilla, has been learning to communicate with people by using American Sign Language (the same sign language used by the deaf). Her teacher is a scientist named Dr. Penny Patterson.

According to Dr. Patterson, Koko has always been interested in cats. She became excited whenever she saw a cat, either a real one glimpsed through the window or a photograph of a cat in a magazine. Finally, Dr. Patterson decided to surprise Koko with a cat of her own. Koko

picked out her own pet, a tailless orange kitten she named "All Ball." Koko frequently used her sign language to tell her trainer how much she loved the kitten. Even though Koko was a giant compared to her tiny pet, she was always gentle and careful not to hurt her.

Then tragedy struck one night when All Ball ran out of the house and was hit by a car. When Dr. Patterson explained in sign language what had happened, Koko was heartbroken. For weeks afterward, she would make the sign "frown-sad" or "cat-sleep" when anyone brought up the subject of cats. She also made a special wailing cry that gorillas use when they are unhappy.

A few months later, Koko had the chance to pick out a new kitten from a litter born at the research station. She was so happy, Dr. Patterson said, that she actually danced when her new pet arrived. Koko is as devoted to the new kitten as she was to All Ball, which goes to show that it isn't just people who can enjoy a special relationship with a pet.

THREE Understanding Your Pet's Behavior

70.
How do cats purr, and what does purring mean?

Scientists have been mystified for years by the cat's purr. It was once thought that vibrations of the blood vessels in the cat's chest caused the sound. It is now thought that cats purr by rapidly contracting and relaxing the muscles in the diaphragm and larynx, which channels the air and creates a low, vibrating sound. A purr can be produced whether the cat is breathing in or out. The talent for purring goes beyond the common house cat—ocelots, cheetahs, and other wild cats do it as well.

No one really knows why cats purr, but since they usually don't do it when they are alone, scientists think it must be a form of communication. Cats also may purr when mating or nursing, or when they are seriously ill. In fact, the only time that cats don't purr is when they are sleeping.

71.
Why do dogs pant?

Dogs pant to cool themselves off. Unlike humans, dogs do not have sweat glands (except for a few in the pads of their feet), so they cannot regulate their body temperature through perspiration. When a dog pants, it takes cool air in through its nose and exhales warm air through its mouth. This helps to keep the dog's body temperature at a normal 101 to 102 degrees Fahrenheit. Because dogs depend on this behavior to survive, it is important, especially in warm weather, never to leave a dog in a hot, confined space. The inside of a car parked in the summer sun can reach 102 degrees in just ten minutes, and a scorching 120 degrees in a half hour, even with the windows partly open. It is easy to see that, when the temperature outside the dog is higher than its body temperature, panting will not help to cool it off. In fact, it will just make things worse. A good rule to follow during the summer is to leave your dog (and your cat) at home in a shady place with plenty of fresh water. If your pet does show signs of heat stroke—rapid panting, twitching, or a wild staring expression—cool the animal down as quickly as possible. One way to do this is to bring the animal into a cool room. If this doesn't help, spray your pet with water or pack ice bags around its head, stomach, and groin. Then call your veterinarian immediately.

72.
Why do cats scratch the furniture?

The most obvious reason that cats scratch furniture, curtains, and scratching posts is to sharpen their claws. But cats may have another reason to scratch, one inherited from their wild relatives. Cats in the wild sometimes scratch tree trunks as a way of marking their territories. The marks on the tree show other cats the territory is occupied. In addition, glands in the cat's paws leave a special scent on the tree that may say to other cats, "I was here."

Though modern-day house cats no longer need to

mark territories, they still scratch. In fact, the behavior is so strong that even cats who have had their claws removed sometimes continue to make scratching motions on furniture and other objects. Because this behavior is so ingrained, it is almost impossible to teach a cat not to do it. Your cat will be happiest if you give it something it enjoys scratching, such as a sturdy post covered with sisal (a ropelike material) or an old tree trunk with the bark still on it. Your parents will be happy if you train your cat to use the post rather than the living room furniture. To do this, put the scratching post near where the cat sleeps—cats usually like to sharpen their claws when they wake up. Each time the cat uses the post, give praise and even a small food treat. If your cat likes catnip, sprinkle some around the post. If you find your cat clawing the furniture, tell it "No!" (but don't yell or scare it). Then pick the cat up and take it over to the scratching post. Before long, your cat should be well trained to mark its territory and sharpen its claws on its special post.

73.
How do dogs mark their territories?

Dogs have very sensitive noses, so it's not surprising to find that they mark their territories with odors. When a male dog insists on stopping at every tree, bush, or hydrant to leave his "calling card," he is, in reality, leaving a message for other dogs who will pass by later. The message says, "I'm a male dog, and this tree (or hydrant) is part of my territory." The next dog to come along picks up the message by sniffing the spot. He can tell, based on the strength of the odor, how recently the first dog was there. The smell may also let him know who the first dog was. If he is feeling dominant, the second dog may decide to lift his own leg on the spot, claiming the territory as his own. Marking by female dogs is very rare.

74.
Why do cats spend so much time licking themselves?

Licking is the cat's way of grooming itself. Cats are very fastidious and spend a great deal of time each day cleaning their fur. The cat's saliva contains a kind of "detergent" that keeps the fur clean and sweet-smelling. The rough tongue also removes dirt and dead hair from the coat.

Keeping clean is especially important for wild cats, whose prey usually have very sensitive noses. A lioness can sneak up on a gazelle much more easily if the gazelle cannot smell her coming.

Licking has other uses in addition to grooming. On hot days, saliva licked onto the fur evaporates and helps to keep the cat cool. Like the dog, the cat has sweat glands only in its feet, so licking is an important way of regulating its body temperature. When the cat's fur is exposed to sunlight, vitamin D is produced. Licking its coat also allows the cat to obtain this important vitamin.

Because it is so flexible, the cat can reach almost every part of its body with its tongue. The only area it cannot lick directly is its head—and the cat solves this problem by licking a paw and using it as a washcloth. Two cats will sometimes help each other out by grooming each other's hard-to-reach places. This happens most often if the two cats are good friends.

75.
What does it mean when a cat wags its tail?

When you see a dog wagging its tail, you can tell that it's feeling friendly. But for cats the same behavior has just the opposite meaning.

Cats switch their tails back and forth when they are angry or annoyed. When you see this behavior, it's a signal that you should leave the cat alone, or risk being scratched or bitten.

Other tail positions say different things. A cat who's feeling happy holds its tail straight up in the air. If it is nervous or cautious it holds its tail low. When it is frightened or angry (when threatened by a strange dog, for example), it tries to make itself look large and menacing by fluffing up the fur on its tail and along its back. The purpose of this display is to convince anyone watching that it is too big and too mean to bother with. You can tell by the way some dogs (and people) respond that they believe the cat's threat!

76.
What should you do if you get a new kitten and your "old" cat won't get along with it?

Sometimes, the solution to this problem is just a matter of introducing the two cats in the right way. Cats, like people, can get jealous of each other. When you bring home a new kitten, your "old" cat may feel insecure and afraid that you don't love it anymore. If you pay a lot of attention to the kitten (as most people do when they get a new pet) your cat will be convinced that it has been replaced. The new kitten is the cause of all its unhappiness, so it is natural that your cat won't be very friendly.

The key to having an old pet accept a new one is to let your first cat know that it is still your favorite. When you take the new kitten home, try to have someone else bring it into the house. If your cat sees you with the newcomer, it will really be angry. Give the kitten a separate food bowl and litter box, so your old cat doesn't feel it has competition. Then, for the first few days, pay as much attention to your old cat as possible, and try to ignore the new kitten. This will be hard to do, but it will reassure your old cat that you still love it and that the kitten is not a threat. Once it understands this, it can afford to be nice, and soon your two cats may be better friends than you ever thought was possible.

77.
What should you do if you are walking your dog and another dog runs up to it?

For many dog owners, this is a frightening situation, because they are afraid the two dogs will get into a fight. But an approaching dog, even if it seems large and threatening, usually isn't ready to attack. Most of the time, all it wants to do is find out who your dog is and say hello.

To understand what is going on, it helps to know how dogs greet each other. When two dogs meet, they approach each other cautiously, sometimes with their ears pricked up and their hackles raised. Next they circle and sniff each other to answer the important questions: Is this a boy or a girl? Is this a dog I know?

Finally, one dog may rest its head or paw across the other's back. After the greeting ritual is completed, both dogs may walk a few paces away to mark a tree or bush.

Why is it, then, that two dogs on leashes (or one dog on a leash who meets a free-roaming dog) often act so aggressive? Part of the reason is that the leash is usually too short to allow the dog to take part in the greeting ritual. If you hold back on the leash so that your dog cannot investigate the other animal, your dog will think something is wrong and become frustrated and aggressive.

The second thing that may cause a fight is, surprisingly, *your* behavior. When you yank on the leash, you're sending a message to your dog that you're afraid, and it may become aggressive in order to protect you.

When your dog meets another dog during a walk, a fight should be the exception rather than the rule. To avoid hostility, hold the leash as loosely as possible to let your dog greet the other dog. Watch for signs of real aggression, such as snarling or teeth-baring. If the dogs do start to fight, drop the leash and don't try to interfere. Your dog will be less likely to keep fighting if it doesn't feel it has to protect you.

78.
Why do dogs bite?

Dogs bite people for a number of different reasons. Many dogs bite when they feel threatened. If you enter the yard of a dog who doesn't know you, it may think you are trying to invade its territory and bite you to convince you to go away. If you disturb a dog who is eating or sleeping, it may also react by biting.

In dog language, a direct stare is a kind of threat. If you stare into the eyes of any dog (but especially a dog that doesn't know you), you may be challenging the animal without realizing it and inviting it to bite you.

Dogs also bite when their "chase response" is triggered. Like wolves and other canines, dogs are hunters. The sight of an animal (or a person) running away stimulates them to chase and bite, just as they would do to bring down a prey animal. In the wild, most dogs hunt in groups, helping each other to capture animals larger than themselves. The actions of each animal help to excite other pack members. This is why dogs in a pack are more likely to attack and bite than are single dogs. It is also why dogs are more apt to bite when they are excited.

Dogs can inflict serious wounds with their bites. The average dog bites down with a force of 150 to 200 pounds per square inch. A trained attack dog can clamp its jaws shut with a force of 400 to 450 pounds per square inch.

79.
How can you avoid being bitten by a dog?

The first step in avoiding a dog bite is to understand *why* dogs bite. Unfortunately, this is something that many people do not understand—an estimated 3 million people in the United States are bitten by dogs each year. (It is hard to know exactly how many dog bites occur, since most people don't go to the doctor or notify the health department when they are bitten.)

Most dog bites are not from stray or wild dogs. In fact, people who get bitten are usually bitten by their own pets or by neighborhood pets.

Once you know what makes dogs bite, it is easy to keep it from happening to you. Because dogs bite when they feel threatened, you should never go into the yard of a dog you don't know. Never try to take food or a toy away from *any* dog, even your own pet. Never try to wake up a dog who is asleep by shaking or poking at it. (The best idea is to pay attention to the old saying and "let sleeping dogs lie.")

What if a dog comes up to you on the street, barking and growling? The worst thing you can do is try to run away (which will trigger the dog's chase response) or start yelling (which will excite it). Instead, stand very still with your arms at your sides. Don't accidentally challenge the dog by looking into its eyes—instead, turn your head and look away. There's a good chance that, after a few minutes, the dog will leave, having decided that you're not a threat after all.

The most important thing is to learn to recognize the body language of a dog who is ready to bite. The signals include growling, barking, baring the teeth, and standing stiff-legged with the tail held straight up.

80.
How should you approach a dog you don't know?

Most dogs are very friendly once they get to know you. But, like people, dogs don't always want to be friends right away. They need time to get acquainted and decide that you're okay.

Don't make the mistake of trying to pet or hug a strange dog. You wouldn't like it if someone you didn't know ran up and hugged you. Most dogs don't like it either.

The first thing to do before you approach a strange dog is to ask the owner's permission. The owner is the best judge of how friendly his or her dog will be. If the owner gives permission, stand still and let the dog come up to you and smell you. Dogs depend heavily on their sense of smell, and sniffing is a dog's way of finding out who you are. Next, make your hand into a fist and slowly extend your arm, holding your hand under the dog's nose. Don't keep your hand open or hold it above the dog's head, or it may think you're going to hit it.

After the dog has had some time to sniff your closed hand, you will probably be able to pet it. Remember, the key to meeting a new dog is to take your time, be gentle, and let the dog be in charge of the introduction.

81.

Why is it necessary to housebreak a puppy, while a kitten will use the litter box without being taught?

One of the biggest differences in the behavior of dogs and cats is in their bathroom habits. Dogs must be taught to "go" outside or on newspapers, rather than anywhere they please. If not trained by their owners, dogs will never learn this important lesson. Cats, on the other hand, seem to know automatically how to use the litter box.

This difference in behavior leads many people to think of cats as being cleaner—and sometimes smarter—than dogs. But the difference has nothing to do with intelligence. Rather, it can be traced back to the life-styles of our pets' wild ancestors.

Dogs in the wild are pack animals. Dog packs often roam and hunt large territories, never settling down in one place for very long. Because they do not have permanent dens, they are not too concerned about keeping their living areas clean. If the den gets dirty, they can always move along to a new home.

Cats, on the other hand, become very attached to particular places. Wild cats often live for long periods of time in the same lair. Thus for cats, or any animal with a permanent home, it is more important to keep that home clean. This may explain the natural tendency of cats to use the litter box and to cover up their droppings.

82.

Why do cats sleep so much?

No one really knows. But it is a fact that cats spend more time asleep than any other mammal. The average cat sleeps away about two-thirds to three-quarters of every day. People sleep only about half as much.

During the day, most of a cat's sleep consists of short "cat naps," when the animal sleeps lightly. In this stage of sleep the cat is actually very alert. Its muscles remain tense and ready for action, and the smallest sound will bring it wide awake.

A cat goes into deep sleep for only about three to four hours every day. This is the stage when animals (and people) dream. In sleep tests, scientists have found that cats sometimes act out their dreams—crouching, grooming themselves, and chasing imaginary mice.

How did the scientists know that the cats they observed were really asleep? Simple. They could tell by looking at the "third eyelid," a thin membrane that slides across the cat's eye, underneath the regular eyelid, when a cat is in deep sleep.

83.
People are either left-handed or right-handed. Are animals left- or right-pawed?

Yes. Like people, certain animals seem to prefer doing things with either their left or their right paw. As you probably know, most people are right-handed.

In cats, it's just the other way around. Most cats are left-pawed. You can test your cat to see if it's right- or left-pawed in the following way:

Using a sheet of stiff paper, make a tube about two inches across. (You can also use an empty tube from a roll of paper towels.) Tape the tube to the floor. After letting your pet explore and become familiar with the tube, put a piece of its favorite food just in front of the tube's open end, where it can easily reach it. After it eats the food, the test begins.

Place another small piece of food just inside the tube, so your cat will have to reach in with its paw to get it. Watch which paw it uses. Repeat the test ten times, keeping track of which paw the cat uses to get the food out of the tube. If it uses its left foot more often, you've got a left-pawed cat. If right, it's right-pawed. If it shows no preference for either paw, your pet is ambidextrous.

84.
Do all cats like to catch mice?

Although most people think that cats and mice are natural enemies, this isn't always so. Cats are not born knowing how to hunt and kill—they have to learn how to do it.

This learning takes place when a kitten is very young. Watching the mother as she brings prey back to the litter teaches the kitten what kind of animals it should hunt. Sometimes the mother cat brings a live animal back and shows her kittens how to kill it. The roughhousing that kittens do with their brothers and sisters also helps by giving them practice in stalking, pouncing, and biting.

It has been discovered that kittens who are raised without mothers or littermates usually do not grow up to be very good hunters. This is because they haven't had a chance to watch and practice.

Whether a cat becomes a good mouser also depends on its experience with mice. If a mouse is raised along with a litter of kittens, the kittens will probably not kill mice when they grow up, because they have learned to think of mice as friends rather than food.

It's a myth that a cat has to be hungry in order to be a good hunter. A well-fed cat is just as likely to catch mice as one who's hungry. This may help explain why some cats catch mice and leave them on the front porch, never bothering to eat them.

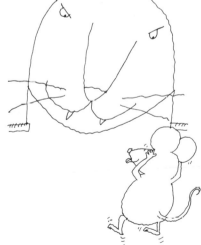

85.

Is it true that a dog or cat will get fat and lazy after it has been "fixed"?

It is a common myth that "fixing" (spaying or neutering) a dog or cat will change the animal's personality and cause it to become fat. Some people also believe that a female dog or cat should have one litter of puppies or kittens before she is spayed.

Neither of these myths is true. Spaying and neutering will not change your pet's personality, except to take away some of the behaviors that people don't like (for males, spraying, chasing after females, and fighting; for females, yowling and crying when in "heat").

It is true that animals don't need to eat quite as much after they have been neutered or spayed. You can keep them from getting fat by feeding them less and making sure they exercise.

Finally, there is no reason for a female dog or cat to have one litter before she is spayed. There are already too many pets who cannot find good homes. Some humane societies estimate that, in the United States alone, 15 million unwanted pets are put to sleep (euthanized) each year, so every litter hurts.

86.

Why does a dog gulp down its food?

If you have a dog, you have probably noticed that, at mealtime, your pet gulps down the food very quickly, hardly stopping to chew. This behavior is probably inherited from the dog's wild ancestors. After a wolf pack brings down a prey animal, all members of the pack must compete for part of the kill. In order to get enough to eat, a wolf must, literally, "wolf" down its food. Even if your dog has plenty to eat and no other dogs to threaten it, its instincts tell it that it must gobble its food in order to survive. These instincts also tell it to snap and growl at anyone who tries to take food away from it. When a dog or wolf wants to take some time to gnaw on a bone, it avoids competition by taking the treat away to eat in private.

87.
Why do cats like to rub against things?

If you have a cat, you've probably noticed its habit of rubbing its head and body against chairs, table legs, and you. You may have thought that your cat was doing this just because it feels good.

While that's undoubtedly part of the reason, it's not the whole story. The contented cat circling around your legs isn't just being friendly—it's also marking you as part of its territory.

Both dogs and cats use odors to brand certain objects as theirs. When your cat rubs against you, special glands in its lips and at the base of its tail deposit its personal scent on you. Through this odor, your cat is leaving a message for other cats that says, "This person is mine!"

88.
Why do dogs and cats turn around in circles before they lie down?

Like many other things that dogs and cats do, circling before lying down is a behavior that goes back to our pets' wild ancestors. When a wild dog or cat prepares to go to sleep, it looks around for a grassy spot. After choosing a place, the animal walks in circles to trample down the long grass, creating a soft, comfortable bed. Even though it's no longer necessary, this behavior is still shown by today's domestic pets.

FOUR   Pets Helping People

89.
Have monkeys ever been trained to help people?

Yes. An experimental program is training capuchin monkeys (the familiar organ-grinder's monkeys) to assist quadriplegics—people who have been paralyzed below the neck or shoulders. The monkeys live with their human companions and can be taught to perform many tasks. These include vacuuming, opening and closing doors, setting up a book on a reading stand, and putting a cassette in a tape player. One monkey helper named Hellion has even been trained to get food from the refrigerator and feed his human companion. While most quadriplegics depend on other people for help, trained capuchin monkeys can make it possible for them to live independently.

90.
Why are dogs used to sniff out bombs, drugs, and missing persons?

The thing that makes dogs so good at these tasks is their incredibly acute sense of smell. While vision is the most important sense for humans, smell is the most important for dogs, and it is likely that dogs live in a world of odors that we cannot even imagine.

In people the olfactory membrane (the smell-sensitive

area inside the nose) is the size of a postage stamp and contains about 5 million receptor cells. In the dog this membrane (if unfolded) would cover an area the size of fifty postage stamps and contains over 200 million receptor cells.

Because they have so many smell receptors, dogs can detect very faint odors. A bloodhound, for example, can follow a person's scent trail by smelling molecules of sweat that have passed through the soles of the person's shoes as he or she walks! And the trail doesn't need to be fresh—bloodhounds have been known to follow scent trails that are several weeks old.

91.
What other things have dogs been trained to do?

The U.S. Customs Service trains dogs to help find shipments of illegal drugs that may enter the country at airports and border crossings. To join the Customs Canine Corps, a dog must have a good temperament and be able to pay attention for long hours. Both mixed breeds and purebreds may apply, but only one in fifty dogs makes it into the training program.

Once selected, the dogs spend at least fourteen weeks at the Canine Training Center in Virginia, where they learn to pick out the odors of marijuana, cocaine, heroin, and other drugs. Equally important, the dogs must learn *not* to respond to the smells of hundreds of substances that are perfectly legal. While the dogs are being trained, human customs agents are also in training, learning to respond to the signals of their future partners.

These canine drug detectors help the Customs Service to do its job faster and better. A dog can check out a suspicious-looking package in seconds—without opening it. And while it would take a human at least twenty minutes to search a car at a border crossing, a dog can investigate it more thoroughly in only five minutes.

A dog's drug-sniffing career lasts about nine years. Afterward, most dogs retire to live out their days as pets of their human partners.

92.
Why are Dalmatians used as "firehouse dogs"?

The popular black-and-white-spotted Dalmatian has a long and interesting history. This breed was originally trained to be a "coach dog." In the 1600s French and British noblemen took along their coach dogs when they made journeys by horse-drawn carriage. The dog's job was to run alongside (or even under) the coach and to protect the travelers from highwaymen and robbers. When the nobleman reached his destination, he often left the dog to guard any valuables in the carriage. Many noblemen thought that the dogs were actually better guards than the coach drivers.

Dalmatians were especially good as coach dogs because they like to run and they are not afraid of horses. These same abilities made them very useful as firehouse dogs in the early 1900s, when fire engines were still pulled by horses. During the early part of this century, almost every firehouse had a Dalmatian, not just as a mascot, but as a working member of the department. The dogs learned to run ahead of the fire engine, barking to warn people to clear the way. Bessie, a famous New York City firehouse dog, used to respond to an alarm by running to the intersection nearest the firehouse and barking to let people know the engine was coming.

When fire departments began the switch to gasoline-powered fire engines, it was bad news for firehouse dogs. The dogs were afraid of the loud motors, and it was dangerous for them to run alongside the big trucks. Though firehouse dogs continued to participate by riding on the engines to the scene of the fire, their working days were over. But the firehouse dog had become a tradition, and even today some fire departments still keep Dalmatians as mascots.

93.
What is a hearing ear dog?

A hearing ear dog gives the same kind of help to a deaf person that a Seeing Eye dog gives to a blind person. Although people with severe hearing loss can lead normal lives, they have trouble with things that most of us take for granted. For example, a deaf person cannot hear a ringing telephone, a doorbell, or an alarm clock. Sometimes these devices are attached to lights that flash on and off when the phone or doorbell rings, but if the person is asleep or in another room, the flashing light doesn't do much good. This is where a hearing ear dog can help.

A hearing ear dog is trained to respond to certain sounds, like doorbells and alarm clocks, by running over to the person it is with, jumping up, and then running back and forth between the person and the sound's source until the person notices. The dog can be taught to respond to many different sounds, depending on the deaf person's needs. For example, some hearing dogs have been taught to react to a baby's cries. This is a big help to a mother who is deaf and cannot hear her child calling her.

94.

What is the most unusual relationship between a person and a pet?

One of the most unusual human-animal relationships is certainly the one between the master cormorant fishermen of Japan and the seabirds who have been trained to catch fish for them. It has long been a tradition in Japan to train cormorants (large seabirds) to help fish for ayu, a troutlike fish that is much prized by the Japanese. Cormorants naturally feed on ayu, so the difficulty is not in training them to catch the fish but in training them to give their catch willingly over to the fishermen.

The Japanese fishermen devote the entire fall and winter to capturing, training, and caring for their birds. Using decoys, the fishermen catch wild sea cormorants when the birds stop on the cliffs of Japan's Honshu Island during their annual migration.

At first the captured birds are very angry and frightened. But after a few weeks of gentle massages, warm baths, and hand feeding by the fishermen, the birds calm down. Before long, they even seem to grow fond of their human captors.

For their part, the fishermen are devoted to the birds. During the winter months, the birds do not work. Instead, they rest and wait for the fishermen to bring them food. Even on the coldest winter days, a fisherman's job is to travel the rivers of Japan, catching carp and catfish to feed his birds. Most nights, the fishermen even sleep outside with their cormorants.

In May, the ayu season opens and it is time for the cormorants to go to work. Every night, each fisherman ventures out with a team of several birds in a small wooden fishing boat. The birds wear a harness and leash made out of cypress bark so that the fisherman can pull them back to the boat or rescue them from dangerous river currents. They also wear a collar around their necks to keep them from swallowing the fish they catch.

A light on the front of the boat attracts a school of ayu and the cormorants go into action. Diving into the river, the cormorants scoop up fish in their large pelicanlike bills. The fisherman uses the leash to tug his birds back to the boat, where they give up their fish, then jump back into the river for more. Amazingly, the birds seem eager to bring the fish back to the fisherman, even though they are not allowed to eat what they catch. Perhaps they are thinking gratefully of those long, cold winters when the tables are turned and they relax while the fisherman works.

95.
Are there any stories of cats helping people?

Yes, and one of the strangest of these comes from ancient Egypt. The Egyptians worshipped cats. Killing a cat was considered such a serious crime that the punishment was death. In 525 B.C., Kambyses, the king of Persia, used the Egyptians' love of cats to help him win a battle against them. Persian troops were attacking the Egyptian city of Pelusium and they seemed to be losing the battle. To turn the tide, Kambyses ordered the Persian soldiers to catch all the cats they could find. Clutching the animals in front of them, the soldiers advanced on the city. The Egyptians didn't dare fire on the Persian soldiers, for fear of injuring the cats. They were forced to surrender, and the city of Pelusium fell to Kambyses.

96.
Have pets ever prevented a disaster?

Although it has never been definitely proved, some scientists believe certain animals know that earthquakes, volcanic eruptions, and other natural disasters are going to take place hours, or even days, before they occur.

There have been several cases where animals have behaved oddly just before major earthquakes. In 1975, Chinese seismologists (scientists who specialize in studying earthquakes) received reports from people in the city of Haicheng that many animals were acting strangely. Based on these and other reports, they decided to evacuate the city. Just twenty-four hours later, a major earthquake hit Haicheng, causing widespread destruction. Because of the animals' predictions, thousands of lives were saved. In 1976, Chinese scientists predicted three other earthquakes, in part by observing the behavior of animals.

Scientists in the United States have also studied the ability of animals to warn humans of natural disasters. A scientist in California set up a hot line and asked volunteers to call in whenever their pets acted strangely. Like the Chinese scientists, he got the most calls just before earthquakes occurred.

Though animal predictions are by no means a foolproof way to forecast earthquakes, it couldn't hurt to keep an eye on your pet's behavior if you live in an earthquake zone.

97.
If animals can predict natural disasters, how do they do it?

People have often thought that animals have some kind of ESP that lets them know when a disaster is about to occur. A more likely explanation, though, is that animals are much more sensitive than people, and that they pick up faint warning signals that humans miss.

Before an earthquake occurs, there are changes in the

electrical activity in the atmosphere. Some scientists think that animals can feel this electrical change as static electricity. Static electricity is what makes your hair stand on end when you rub an inflated balloon over your head. It is also what gives you a shock when you walk across a carpet and touch a doorknob. Because animals are covered with fur, they are much more sensitive than we are to static electricity, and they may become very uncomfortable just before an earthquake hits.

Another idea is that animals, with their very acute hearing, pick up the high frequency sounds of shattering rock that may come before an earthquake or volcanic eruption. They may also detect very tiny tremors in the earth, vibrations too small to be noticed by humans.

It is known that certain animals, including some birds and fish, are sensitive to the earth's magnetic field. Perhaps they feel small changes in this magnetic field before an earthquake (something the most sensitive human could never do), which would explain their "mysterious" ability to predict natural disasters.

98.
Who was the first Seeing Eye dog?

The first Seeing Eye dog in the United States was a female German shepherd named Buddy. She was born in the 1920s at a kennel in Switzerland where her mistress, Dorothy Harrison Eustis, was raising and training German shepherds for police work.

Dorothy Eustis never dreamed she would end up training guide dogs for the blind. In fact, in the 1920s, almost no one had thought of using dogs for this purpose. Then she happened to visit a kennel in Germany where an experiment was being done to teach dogs to aid some of the soldiers blinded in World War I. Mrs. Eustis was so fascinated by the idea of dogs for the blind that she wrote an article about it for the *Saturday Evening Post*. Her article caught the attention of Morris Frank, a young blind man in Tennessee. He wrote to Mrs. Eustis, who invited him to travel to Switzerland to learn to work with one of her dogs.

For five weeks, Morris and Buddy worked together. By the end of their training Morris was able to walk to town on his own for the first time in his life. Buddy and Morris became fast friends, and on several occasions she saved his life, once by dragging him out of the path of a team of runaway horses.

Morris Frank was thrilled with his new freedom. More than anything, he wanted to bring this freedom to other blind people.

Morris and Buddy returned by ship to the United States in 1928. When they got off the boat in New York City, Morris astonished waiting reporters by crossing a busy street with only Buddy's help. As a result of this feat, thousands of people heard about Morris and Buddy. There was so much public interest that, in 1929, Dorothy Eustis returned from Switzerland to found the first guide dog training school in the United States. The school she started, The Seeing Eye, was in New Jersey. Since then, The Seeing Eye and other schools have trained thousands of dogs and blind people to work together.

99.
What's the most amazing story of a human-animal friendship?

Bobby, a Skye terrier who lived in the 1800s, was probably history's most devoted pet. Bobby was the best friend of a Scottish shepherd named John Gray. When John Gray died in 1858, he was buried in Greyfriars Churchyard in

Edinburgh, Scotland. The day after the funeral, Bobby appeared at his master's grave. He stayed there, sleeping on the grave each night, for the next fourteen years. His story was told around the world, and tourists flocked to the churchyard to see the amazing little dog, who became known as Greyfriars Bobby. Bobby died in 1872 and was buried next to John Gray in the churchyard. Today a bronze statue of Bobby, which sits atop a drinking fountain for dogs, has become an Edinburgh landmark.

100.
Has a dog ever been responsible for saving human lives?

In the winter of 1925, an Alaskan malamute named Balto helped to save the lives of the people of Nome, Alaska. An outbreak of diphtheria had hit the isolated town, and the only thing that could bring the epidemic under control was a drug that was not available in Nome. Because of a bad snowstorm, airplanes could not fly into Nome, so the drug had to be brought there by teams of sled dogs.

It was Gunnar Kasson's dog team that made the last leg of the 650-mile journey, with Balto as the lead dog. Subfreezing temperatures and high winds made the going nearly impossible. Huge drifts of snow completely obscured the trail in some sections. Kasson said later that he had no idea where they were. But somehow Balto sensed the trail, leading the pack over snowbanks and across fields of ice until they finally arrived at Nome in the early morning hours of February 2, 1925. To commemorate his bravery, New York City erected a statue of Balto in Central Park, where it still stands today.

101.

Has there ever been a dog in space?

Yes. In fact, the very first space traveler was a dog!

In November 1957, the Russians launched Sputnik II, one of the earliest man-made objects to orbit the Earth. Alone inside the space capsule was a female Samoyed named Laika.

The reason for Laika's trip was to gather information about life in space. Sensors attached to her body measured her heartbeat, breathing, and movements in the weightless environment of the capsule. This information was beamed to scientists on Earth, over one thousand miles away, by powerful radio transmitters.

Laika did very well during her ten-day trip, adapting to weightlessness with no bad effects. Her success as a space traveler helped convince scientists that other animals, and eventually people, would be able to travel safely in space. So, in a way, Laika paved the way for modern-day space travel.

INDEX

ANN SQUIRE, who holds a Ph.D. in animal behavior from the City University of New York, has studied the behavior of a variety of animals, including rats and electric fish. She is currently Vice President for Education at the American Society for the Prevention of Cruelty to Animals in New York City, where she supervises a wide-ranging animal awareness education program. Dr. Squire has written extensively on animal issues.

G. BRIAN KARAS is the illustrator of *The Great Potato Book* and *The Scoop on Ice Cream*. He is also a magazine illustrator and has created a line of greeting cards. He lives in Phoenix, Arizona.

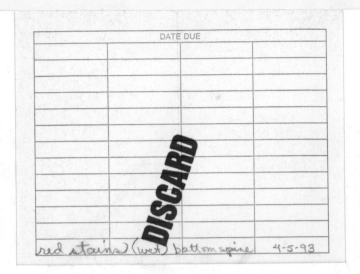